Wispy

Misty

To Calvin: This book wouldn't be possible
without your youthful wisdom and humor. I love you!
—D.D.

To Joshua, one of the sweetest little guys under the sun
—A.K.

For Devon and Ethan, our rays of sunshine
—R.B.

Copyright © 2022 by Dylan Dreyer
Jacket art and illustrations by Rosie Butcher

All rights reserved. Published in the United States by Random House Children's Books,
a division of Penguin Random House LLC, New York.

Random House and the colophon are registered trademarks of Penguin Random House LLC.

Visit us on the Web! rhcbooks.com

Educators and librarians, for a variety of teaching tools, visit us at RHTeachersLibrarians.com

Library of Congress Cataloging-in-Publication Data is available upon request.
ISBN 978-0-593-18042-6 (trade) — ISBN 978-0-593-18044-0 (lib. bdg.) — ISBN 978-0-593-18043-3 (ebook)

MANUFACTURED IN CHINA
10 9 8 7 6 5 4 3 2 1
First Edition

Misty the Cloud

Friends Through Rain or Shine

Dylan Dreyer

with **Alan Katz**

illustrations by
Rosie Butcher

Random House  New York

It was an extra-special day for an extra-special celebration. Clare had waited for what felt like forever for her birthday, and it was finally here!

Her mom was helping her decorate for the big party.
Clare thought the backyard looked perfect.

"But why do I have to share my party with Tyler?"
Clare asked, eyeing her little brother.

"Because his birthday is also coming up. We can
have one huge party with two huge cakes!" her mom said.

(Clare had gotten a peek at her
rainbow cake earlier that morning—
it certainly was huge!)

"Okay, but . . . the little kids have to stay over there. I don't want them messing up my side of the party!"

Way up high in the town of Horizon, Misty the Cloud was also celebrating her birthday. She was very happy to have all her friends at her party—they made the day extra special.

"Pin the Dial on the Compass is so much fun!" Misty said. "We should play again!"

But Misty's mom had another idea; she suggested they go outside for a little while.

"Okay, Mom," Misty said. "Come on, everyone. Let's go play One, Two, Three, Can't Catch Me!"

"Great idea!" her friend Wispy agreed. "I love water games!"

The clouds were having a splashingly good time. But . . .

. . . the water from their game was drizzling down to earth!

Clare and her mother felt the raindrops.

"Oh no!" Clare said.
"What about my party?"

"And mine?" asked Tyler.

"It's just a little sun-shower," their mom said. "Shouldn't last too long."

Meanwhile, up in the sky, the clouds had drifted over to where some sunbeams were playing.

"Do you mind playing *over there*?" said Raye, one of the sunbeams. "Your showers are messing up our game of Funny Sunny."

Misty thought about it. "Well, you could join our game instead," she offered.

Raye shook her head no.
Misty could feel herself getting frustrated.
"But why?" Misty asked.

"You know we're not good at One, Two, Three, Can't Catch Me!
We're sunbeams and we can't make water! Besides, this is where
we *always* play Funny Sunny," Raye said.

"Yes, but this is where we always play *our* game. Plus, it's my birthday and I'm having fun!" Misty told her.

"Me too!" Scud added.
"Me twelve!" Nimby giggled.

I think you mean "three."

"Mom, it's *still* raining!" Clare complained.
"Yes, but look at all the great mud it's making!"
Tyler said as he splashed his truck into a big puddle.

Their mom hoped the rain would stop for Clare's sake, but she agreed the mud was perfect for all the toys Tyler had brought to the yard. She smiled.

But nobody was smiling in Horizon.

The clouds and the sunbeams continued their separate games,
but they were totally in each other's way.

It wasn't fun for anyone.

"They should beam their sunshine someplace else!" Misty insisted.

"Well, I think the *clouds* should go sprinkle someplace else!" Raye said.

"It's my party, and I'll rain if I want to!" Misty told her.
There seemed to be no answer. And then Misty softly said, "Unless . . ."

"Unless *what*?" Raye asked.
"Unless we play a game we're *all* good at—like Rain or Shine!"

Raye considered Misty's suggestion.
She *did* love Rain or Shine, and the
thought brightened her mood.
"That's a great idea!" Raye beamed.

As the clouds and sunbeams darted across the sky together,
Wispy noticed something special happening.

"Misty! Raye! Check it out!"
Misty and Raye looked down and saw . . .

. . . that they had created the most spectacular rainbow ever!

Everyone agreed that finding a way to get along was a beautiful thing.

"Look at that! When we rain *and* shine, we're pretty amazing!" Kelvin pointed out.

Misty cheered.
So did Raye.

"Mom! Clare! Look up!" Tyler called out.

"Wow, what a beautiful rainbow!" Clare exclaimed.

"The perfect decoration for my party!"

"And *mine*!" Tyler said.

The rainbow had shown up just in time.
Their guests were starting to arrive.

The colors in the sky made Tyler's friends want to play with all the crafts Clare had set out.

Tyler sat down with them—and started painting a picture of a muddy truck.

And the puddles drew Clare's friends to Tyler's part of the backyard. She ran over to join the fun.

"Hey, Tyler," she called to him. "Can I borrow your shovel?"

"Of course!" he told her.

Everyone was enjoying themselves in Horizon, too.

Once Misty and Raye agreed that having fun together was a great idea, they had the best afternoon playing . . .

Rain or Shine

Climate Climb-It

Sun-Shower Sprint

Avoid the Asteroid

In Clare and Tyler's backyard, it wasn't just her party. And it wasn't just his.
It was *their* party.
Together.

And thanks to the good times up in Horizon, the forecast was for a perfect mix of sun and clouds, all day long!

Some Weather Facts and Fun from Dylan!

HI, EVERYONE! I'M VERY EXCITED TO INTRODUCE YOU TO MY FRIEND ROY G. BIV.

THAT'S ME!

HIS NAME IS VERY SPECIAL! LOOK!

RED

ORANGE

YELLOW

GREEN

BLUE

INDIGO

VIOLET

WHITE

White is actually made up of all the colors of the rainbow.
And the first letters of those colors spell out Roy's name!

A rainbow is an *optical illusion* that occurs when white light is *refracted* and *reflected* through raindrops.

Know Your Weather Terms

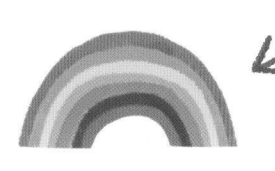

Rainbow
An optical illusion of light and water in the atmosphere. Occurs when sunlight is dispersed through droplets of water.

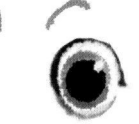
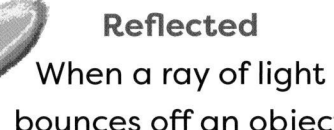

Optical Illusion
When something appears to be something else. For example, a rainbow looks like many colors but is really dispersed white light.

Refracted
When a ray of light bends as it moves through something, such as water or glass

Reflected
When a ray of light bounces off an object

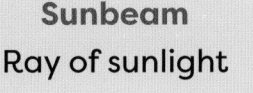

Sunbeam
Ray of sunlight

GOOD THING WE DECIDED TO PLAY TOGETHER, BECAUSE WE'RE BOTH IMPORTANT!

Benefits of Sunshine

★ Helps plants grow.
★ Keeps people and animals healthy.
★ Improves everyone's mood.

Benefits of Clouds and Rain

★ Clouds provide shade on hot days.
★ Rain waters the flowers.
★ Rain fills lakes, streams, and oceans.

Activity

Create a Rainbow at Home!

Turn off the lights. Place a mirror in a glass of water, and shine a light into the mirror. Then hold up a piece of white paper. You'll see a rainbow!

Rain can create a rainbow, but so can:

Mist

Fog

Ice crystals

Even water from a hose!

Did You Know?

A rainbow is actually a full circle, but the horizon cuts our view in half!

A Place Where Hurricanes Happen

by Renée Watson ❖ illustrated by Shadra Strickland

RANDOM HOUSE 🏠 NEW YORK

We're from New Orleans,
a place where hurricanes happen.
But that's only the bad side.

Adrienne

Playing outside is my favorite thing to do.
I play with my friends
Keesha, Michael and Tommy,
who live down the block.
Our favorite game is hide-and-go-seek.
No one can ever find me.
I hide in the best places.
Keesha is easy to find.
She hides behind the same tree every time—
the one in front of Michael's house.
Always giggling to herself
'cause she thinks she's tricked us.

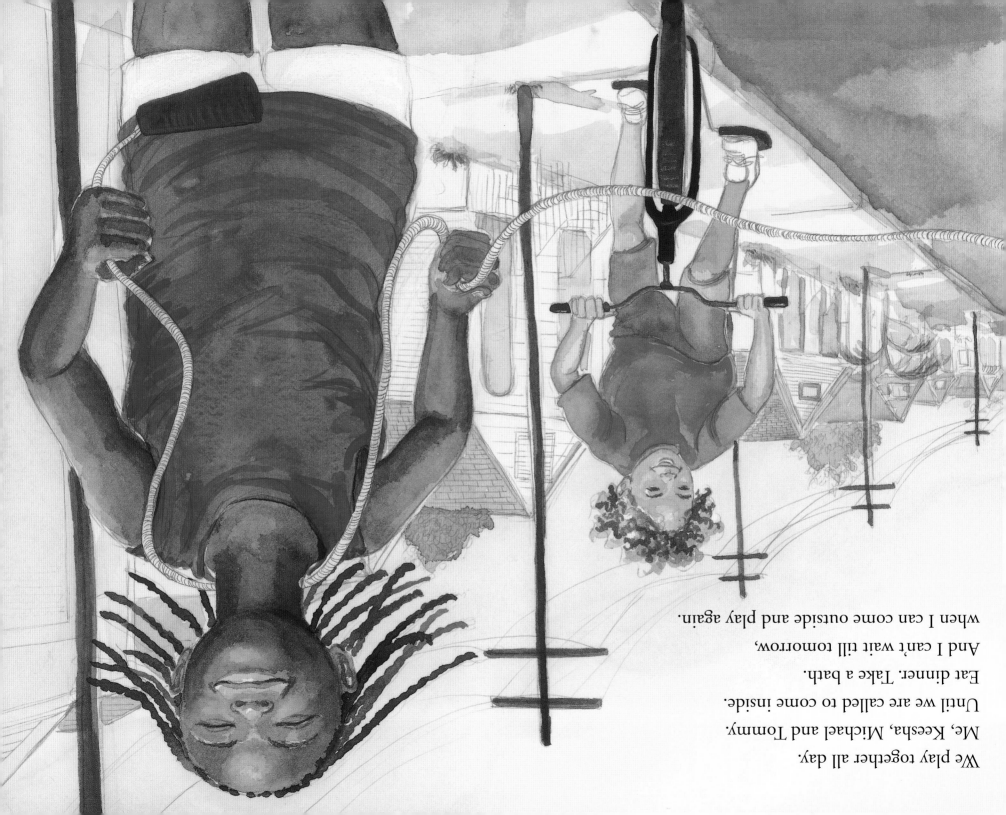

We play together all day.
Me, Keesha, Michael and Tommy.
Until we are called to come inside.
Eat dinner. Take a bath.
And I can't wait till tomorrow,
when I can come outside and play again.

Michael

Jasmine is my little sister.
She is six. I am eight.
I get to do more things than her
because I am the oldest.
I am the one who makes sure Jasmine doesn't get hurt
when we go outside to play.

I am the one who can walk down the block all by myself.
I am the one who picks Jasmine up from her babysitter's house.
As I walk down the street, I see my neighbors on their porches.
My ears are full of gospel, hip-hop and jazz
blasting from car stereos.
Everybody says hello on my block
and I say hello back, even if I don't know their names.

When I get to Mrs. Johnson's house,
she has a cold glass of sweet tea waiting for me.
We sit on Mrs. Johnson's porch, drinking our tea
and adding to the puzzle she's working on.
When it's time to go, I take Jasmine's hand
and hold it the whole way home
because that is what big brothers do.